Wings of Olympus

THE COLT OF THE CLOUDS

Wings of Olympus

of

THE COLT OF THE CLOUDS

BY

KALLIE GEORGE

HARPER

An Imprint of HarperCollinsPublishers

Author's Note

Throughout this book, in most names, "k" is used instead of a "c," as that is the Greek form of spelling, whereas a "c" would be Roman. However, Hercules we have here spelled with a "c" because it is the most commonly used version of the hero's name.

Wings of Olympus: The Colt of the Clouds
Text copyright © 2020 by Kallie George
Illustrations copyright © 2020 by Celia Krampien
All rights reserved. Printed in the United States of America. No part of this book
may be used or reproduced in any manner whatsoever without written permission except in
the case of brief quotations embodied in critical articles and reviews. For information address
HarperCollins Children's Books, a division of HarperCollins Publishers, 195 Broadway,
New York, NY 10007.
www.harpercollinschildrens.com
ISBN 978-0-06-274156-1
Typography by Joe Merkel
21 22 23 24 25 PC/BRR 10 9 8 7 6 5 4 3 2 1
❖
First paperback edition, 2021

To Orion, named after the stars—K. G.

*I*n a cave thick with shadows, in the deepest depths of Mount Olympus, she sat restlessly on her throne, her wings wrapped around her. It was not yet night, and for her this meant a chance to sleep. But she couldn't. Something was bothering her.

Someone was bothering her.

He stood before her and bowed, humbly. They were all humble before her—all the other gods and goddesses—for she had been there long before they were even born. Why, she had birthed the gods—at least, a good many of them.

"Help me," he pleaded.

"Why should I help you?" she replied.

"Because . . ." He reached into his chiton, shimmering like an abalone shell, and pulled out a feather, presenting it to her. It was long and silver and bright as a star. A feather from Pegasus, the first winged horse, who had long since retired to the night sky as one of her constellations. "Because of this."

She took the feather thoughtfully. She imagined them all, how dazzling her cloak would be, far brighter than her daughter's. And though she had vowed never to work for anyone but herself, she surprised herself with her answer.

"So be it," she said.

One

Above the rolling fields of Thessaly, clouds wisped across the sky like horses' tails. In the distance, toward Mount Olympus, Pippa could see darker, thicker ones gathering, but she didn't pay them any attention, too focused on the task at hand.

She hoisted another rock to fill in the hole in the pasture wall, wiping her hands on her *chiton*. She knew she shouldn't dirty it, but sometimes she forgot. It's why she preferred a short tunic rather than this chiton or the fancy embroidered *peplos* that Helena liked her to wear.

"You don't have to help me with this," said Bas, wiping sweat from his brow. The sun was still shining, despite the hint of a coming storm.

"I want to," Pippa said. It was this or lessons. Helena, Bas's mother, was waiting for her to continue with their weaving before she had to oversee supper preparations. Pippa would rather lift a thousand rocks than twist and tangle her fingers in yarn. She wished she were better at it like Bas's sisters, or at least liked it better. But she didn't. And that made things worse.

"Well, we're almost done anyway," said Bas, then added ruefully, "until the next time."

The wild horses had broken the fence more than once now to get to the old stables, unused except for storing surplus hay. Pippa didn't really mind. She liked the wild horses that streaked free across the sun-washed hills of Thessaly, their bodies small and sturdy, their manes and tails tangled with twigs and leaves.

She had seen them only a handful of times when she was out riding with her horse, Zephyr, but was pleased whenever she did. They didn't have wings like Zeph once had, yet they were special too, and carried themselves with the same pride.

"*Feral* horses, not wild," Bas's father liked to correct. "They ran away from a farm like mine, years and years ago."

But to Pippa, they were wild—wild and free.

"Done," declared Bas, putting the last piece of rubble in place.

The fence looked taller than before, stretching seemingly without end along the rolling pasture. In the distance, Pippa could see Zeph grazing, his silvery-white tail swishing rhythmically. Farther away were the other horses. They liked to keep their distance from Zeph, although so far he had caused no problems, not even with the mares. Beyond the horses was the *oikos*, the house, its sunbaked brick glowing golden in the afternoon light.

Pippa glanced at Bas and understood his proud smile.

After she had returned with him from the race on Mount Olympus and had seen it all for the first time—the pastures, the stables, the grand house with its courtyard big enough to enclose an olive tree—she knew at once how wealthy Bas's family must be. Only the wealthy, the *hoi aristoi*, could afford horses. Suddenly, she had been afraid to meet his family. Would they really want to take in a foundling like her, especially one with a horse to feed as well?

"I have plenty of sisters. What's one more?" Bas had said reassuringly. "My family will love you. You have a way with horses."

She *did* have a way with horses. But people were more of a puzzle. Bas was one of her two true friends, along with Sophia, who had won the Winged Horse Race and now lived on Mount Olympus with the gods.

Still, Pippa needn't have worried. Bas had been right; his family had welcomed her with open arms. To them, she wasn't a foundling, she was a rider, chosen by Aphrodite, the goddess of love. And Zeph—he was a winged horse. Even without his wings, he was instantly a legend. So everything was fine. At least, at first. . . .

Bas ran his hand through his dark hair. "I should find my father and tell him we're done." He paused. "Are you coming?"

"In a bit," said Pippa, gazing fondly back at Zeph.

Bas gave her a reproachful look. "You're thinking of riding, aren't you?"

Pippa shook her head.

But, of course, that's exactly what she was thinking.

* * *

The moment Bas was out of sight, Pippa hurried to the stables to pocket some figs. They were Zeph's favorite. If she was quick, she and Zeph could be back before the storm. Helena wouldn't have time to notice that Pippa was gone.

When she reached Zeph out in the pasture, he was as eager as she. His silver tail was lifted high and seemed to float in the wind. His forelock stuck up too, like a tiny horn, and she smoothed it down. She hadn't brought a saddlecloth or reins. With Zeph, she didn't need any.

Quickly, she vaulted onto his back, a move that took strength but had become second nature for Pippa. Then they were off.

They rode past the fields of olive trees and barley that grew green and gold beside the river. Past the vineyards, where the grapevines were just beginning to bud. Past the other farmhouses that glowed with the last slips of sun. Soon they entered the small town and the *agora*, the marketplace, where lyre music filled the air and servants and slaves haggled with traders and stallholders over the price of cheese and olives, eggs and bread. Children scurried by—laughing, rolling hoops with sticks, and pulling each other in toy chariots—but when they saw Pippa and Zeph, they stopped to stare and whisper. Everyone in town knew about her and Zephyr, the winged horse without wings.

In the center of town, on a rise, Pippa could see the temple built to honor Zeus, king of the gods, although none but the oracles and priests could go there. Soon, she'd passed through the town and was back into the countryside, the cobblestone road turning to dirt.

The sun warmed her cheeks, and she breathed in the sweet, fresh smell of river and earth, horse and hay. Nearby, the water lapped at the river's banks. The gentle *clip-clop* of Zeph's hooves and lullaby swish of his tail made Pippa beam with pleasure. There was nothing she wouldn't do for him.

She pressed her legs into his sides, coaxing him to gallop quickly by the hut of the old crone Leda, who watched everything with the acuity of Argus, the many-eyed giant. If Leda saw Pippa pass, she would no doubt report to Helena as soon as she could. There were lots of old women in the village, but none as grouchy as Leda. No one knew much about her, except to stay away. Although she loved to poke into other people's business, she kept her own past as hidden as her hair beneath her *himation*, the woolen cloak that she never left the house without.

Before long they came to a fork in the path. One way led to the next town, the other toward the hills.

"To the hills," Pippa decided aloud. She had spent many an hour exploring the forests in this area, and the way to the hills was prettiest.

She knew she should head back, but the sooner she returned, the sooner the lessons began. Missing a lesson meant more weaving and spinning the next day. There was no avoiding it.

She tightened her grip on Zeph's mane. He snorted, and his shoulders shuddered in a strange way that only his did. Often Pippa wondered if he was still trying to flex his wings. She had watched him carefully those first few weeks after he had lost them to see how much he missed flying. But even now he seemed, two years later, to be happy.

But was she?

Before she had a chance to think further on this, the ground shook and a loud crack filled the air. *Thunder.*

Pippa glanced at the sky. The thick, dark clouds were directly overhead now, so it almost felt like night but starless. Again thunder cracked, this time so loud it made Pippa jump. Zeph froze, his ears pricked.

When the thunder was this mighty, Zeus had to be near. Pippa searched the sky for a lightning bolt, for a flash of wing or hoof. But there was nothing. No sign of Zeus, or his winged steed, Ajax, the winner of the most recent Winged Horse Race.

Pippa sighed, as Zeph, his ears still on the alert, continued along the path to the meadows of blossoms and stones. She would love to see a winged horse again. All she had was a single feather she'd kept from Zeph's wings. She had gotten the idea from Zeus, who kept a feather from Pegasus, his first winged steed, pinned on his cloak.

It seemed so long ago now since the race. She wasn't sure if Zeph missed flying, but she did.

It was a secret she told no one, not even Bas. He wouldn't understand. He hadn't wanted to stay on Mount Olympus. He had missed his family too much. Besides, there was nothing she could do about how she felt. She and Bas had been banished from the mountain, from the winged horses. That was their punishment for having cheated, switching horses on the morning of the race.

And there was no hope of her being chosen for the

Winged Horse Race again, since not only was she banished but also the race occurred only once every hundred years. Maybe her daughter—no, granddaughter . . . But that meant Pippa would have to marry, and then she'd spend even more time weaving and cooking and washing, all the things that women were supposed to do. All the things she had never learned because she had no mother. She bit her lip. This was the reason for the lessons from Helena. Bas had lessons too, only his were with a tutor who taught him how to read and write.

Pippa could just imagine her friend Sophia being outraged at the difference. Sophia loved books and studying more than anything. Now that she was a demigoddess on Mount Olympus, she could take part in lessons with boys. She could *teach* boys, for that matter.

Sometimes Pippa wondered if all Bas's sisters really were as pleased with their places in life as they made out to be. If they weren't, they didn't share it with her. She certainly knew that Astrea, the youngest, loved horses almost as much as she did and was often found playing in the stables, much to Helena's dismay.

Pippa sighed and stuck her hand in the pocket of her peplos, touching her coin, the only thing she had left from her parents. They'd abandoned her when she was a baby. For a long time, Pippa had thought the coin—silver with a winged horse on it—was an *obolos*, a coin that was given to those left for dead, as fare for safe passage into the Underworld. But Aphrodite, who had been Pippa's patron during the race, had confirmed that it wasn't. It was a symbol of good luck; it meant she was loved. It was also a reminder that she was different. She should have insisted that Aphrodite find out more about her parents. Why had they abandoned her? But you couldn't insist upon anything when it came to the gods and goddesses. They did as they pleased.

Like now. What was Zeus up to?

The clouds roiled overhead, more turbulent than she'd ever seen. As the first few drops of rain fell, they tingled on her skin, making it prickle.

Strange, thought Pippa.

She stuck out her tongue to taste the droplets, only to snap it back in at once. This *wasn't* ordinary rain. It was salty!

Two

The rain poured down harder—great big drops—
pooling and puddling, soaking Pippa's hair and
dripping from Zeph's mane. Pippa tested it again,
licking the water from her hand, just to make sure.
Salty!

Storms didn't make salty rain. Something was
wrong. She shivered and looked up at the sky again,
trying to spot Zeus. But there was no sign of him, only
huge black clouds that looked like bruises in the sky.

"Come on, Zeph. Time to go home," Pippa said,
tugging on his mane.

But Zeph wouldn't move. His ears were pricked and his muscles taut.

"Come on," Pippa urged again. But instead of turning back toward the stables, he did the opposite, stepping forward, his ears swiveling this way and that, as though he could hear something she couldn't.

"No, Zeph," said Pippa, this time pressing her legs into his sides.

But her horse wouldn't listen. He took another step along the path.

Boom! The sound split the air and set the ground shaking with a force that felt more like an earthquake than thunder. Zeph reared, and Pippa tipped backward.

"Whoa!" she cried, pressing her body forward and frantically wrapping her arms around his neck.

When Zeph came down on all four feet, he took off, bolting along the path, his hooves churning the flooded earth to mud, and it took all Pippa's strength just to hang on. Her body slipped against his in the rain, and she could barely see as the salty drops drilled her eyes. He galloped so fast he seemed almost to hover, as though he had found his wings again.

The path twisted along the riverside, and soon the meadows turned to trees. Zeph sped between the pines and laurels, their branches trembling from the force of the deluge.

"Stop!" Pippa cried, but Zeph was like a different horse, a wild one who wouldn't listen to her, who didn't even know her.

Pippa knew he wasn't perfect. He was an easily distracted horse. That was why he was named after a zephyr, a breeze, because, as a winged horse, he had often darted and dallied like one. But he had never moved in such a determined, driven way, except perhaps during the race itself.

The branches flew by overhead, nearly knocking her off his back.

Enough was enough! She *had* to stop him.

She pulled back as hard as she could on his mane, but Zeph only shot forward faster, and this time Pippa couldn't keep her hold. She slid off, tumbling to the earth. She curled her body and landed on her side. *Thump!* Luckily, the muddy ground softened her fall.

Instantly, she sprang up. Zeph was already a silvery speck, streaking through the trees, blurred by the pouring rain.

"ZEPH!" she shouted. She ran after him, leaping over branches and roots of trees. The forest was dark and empty, as though the storm had frightened all the animals—the birds and boars and many others—into hiding.

Another boom of thunder shook the sky, and again the ground quaked. Pippa clutched a tree branch to keep her footing. A storm didn't cause earthquakes or salty rain. This was the gods expressing their anger. But at whom? She prayed to Aphrodite to keep her and Zeph safe.

Pippa was soaked now, her hair dripping into her eyes, her chiton sticking to her body. "Zeph! Zeph!" she cried. She listened but could hear only the pounding of the rain.

"ZEPH!" she cried again.

Was that a distant whinny?

She pressed on, through the trees, in the mud.

She heard the sound once more. It *was* a whinny. High-pitched and desperate.

Was he hurt?

"ZEPH!" she cried, her voice wobbling.

She ran even faster, slipping and falling and slipping again. Until, at last, the trees opened up and she emerged into a clearing.

Zeph!

Pippa let out a huge sigh of relief. She had found him! He wasn't hurt. There he circled, his coat slick with rain, in front of an old temple.

Pippa had heard of this old temple to Zeus, but she had never seen it, despite her many outings through the hills. The new one had been built long before she came to Thessaly.

Once, the temple might have been impressive and imposing, but now it looked anything but. Vines and moss grew between thickly between the columns. The roots of an oak tree had pushed up the stone steps, causing them to crumble. Gold and silver paint was peeling from the walls. And, worse, a column had collapsed inward on part of the roof, creating a mountain of white rubble. The damage looked recent, perhaps even caused by the storm.

Zeph paced and pawed, whinnying frantically.

All of a sudden, Pippa knew why.

From inside the temple, another horse whinnied back.

Three

Pippa's breath caught in her throat.

She stepped closer, until she was beside Zeph. She couldn't see the strange horse fully through the rubble and the relentless rain. Only a flash of silver mane and tail. A wild horse—it had to be! It must have been seeking shelter inside when the temple collapsed. Surely it could push its way through the vines on the other side. Unless it was trapped.

But then it gave another whinny—more like a shriek this time—and Pippa knew: it was panicked. A panicked horse was like a panicked person. Logic was forgotten.

Zeph turned to Pippa, snorting anxiously.

"How did you know?" Pippa asked. Zeph's starry eyes bore into hers, not answering, only pleading.

"Hush!" she cried to the horse, though she knew her words wouldn't help. She needed to *do* something.

She began to shift the rubble. The stones were hard to move, wet and slippery in the rain. Pippa managed to lift the first few, then roll some others out of the way. *Thud!* They fell, heavy, in the muck outside the temple. When a piece of stone was too big for Pippa to move on her own, Zeph helped, using his nose to push it aside.

Pippa talked to the horse as she worked, even though the roar of the rain drowned out her voice. "Shhh, shhh," she said, huffing. "It's okay."

At last, they'd cleared a hole just big enough for the horse to get out. She peered inside, but it was too dark and shadowy to see much.

"Here, come here," called Pippa as reassuringly as she could. "You're free now."

Zeph nickered as though repeating her words.

The horse snorted. Zeph did too. A small silver nose reached out to touch his.

Pippa let out a long, soft whistle and held out her

hand. The little horse took a step backward into the shadows. Pippa remembered the figs that she had pocketed for Zeph. She pulled one out and offered it.

Zeph snorted eagerly.

"Not for you," she chided.

She waited patiently, and at last the silver nose appeared again, followed by a face. Its nostrils flared out, wide and round as two *drachma* coins, and its ears flicked back and forth furiously. Its eyes were a deep, dreamy black, just like Zeph's but even blacker, if that was possible. It sniffed, and slowly . . . very slowly . . . it nosed her hand.

Its muzzle was soft, soft as clouds.

"Come on," she coaxed. As slow as sunbeams move across a meadow, the colt—for it *was* a colt—stepped out of the temple.

Buffeted by the rain and wind, the colt's whole body trembled, from his long legs and knobby knees to his . . .

Pippa gasped.

Wings. Two wings rose from his back, spindly and silver, with dustings of gold glittering like a starry sky. They were half folded, like delicate fans, but huge. Rain dripped from the long feathers, pooling at his hooves.

Winged horses weren't supposed to roam below Mount Olympus. It was a rule. That's why Zeph had lost his wings on the way down. Long ago, Bellerophon, on a quest to become a hero, had tamed Pegasus with a golden bridle, but when he had tried to ride the winged horse up to the palace of the gods, he'd nearly died. Bellerophon was now the immortal groom of Mount Olympus. But since then, no winged horses had touched mortal soil.

Until now.

Though the colt's wings were huge, the rest of him was small. He wasn't fully grown, although he wasn't as small as a foal either. A yearling, too old to need his mare but still too young to be by himself. He wasn't alone now. Zeph nosed the colt again, leaning his head down tenderly.

All at once, Pippa thought of the fence and the wild horses. So many times they had broken through. Maybe one of the mares had been breaking in for a reason—to see Zeph. It was the only explanation. And also explained why he was so eager to help. This was his *son*.

And his son was hurt.

Pippa's heart thrummed. She felt a surge of protective love.

She could see that the colt's left wing looked strange, held closer to his side than his right one. He was injured. Had a rock fallen on him?

"It's okay, little one," she said. She couldn't let him stay here; she had to bring him back. He needed a good meal—barley mash with beans—and someone to look after his injured wing. The rain still pummeled the earth.

She didn't have a lead rope, but she did have her belt, a long, thin piece of cloth that held her chiton in place. She took it off and tied a simple loop.

The colt retreated slightly, so she stuck her hand into the pocket of her chiton to get another fig.

She dropped it on the soggy ground. The colt sniffed and took a step forward. Quickly, he munched it up. His ears perked.

With a simple flick, Pippa tossed the rope around his neck.

He didn't like that. He pulled back, his ears flat against his head. Despite his small size, he nearly pulled her over. She planted both feet as firmly as she could on the slippery soil.

Zeph nudged the colt and gave a comforting whinny, which helped calm him down enough so Pippa could pull out the last fig.

"That's all I have," she said. "But there are more back at the stables."

The colt snorted again. He must have been in pain. Yet his enormous eyes, framed in long lashes, showed a sense of curiosity, just like his father.

Pippa held the rope carefully as she climbed on Zeph's back. "Come on," she said to him gently.

Of course, the colt was not used to people, and the temple had just collapsed around him. . . .

But she would look after him. He was Zeph's colt, after all. She promised—promised the sky, and the gods and goddesses, and the colt himself. She knew just what to name him. "*Tazo*," she whispered. It meant *to promise*.

Four

The rain continued to fall as, together, Pippa, Zeph, and Tazo began the long walk back home.

The smell of salt hung heavy in the air. It reminded Pippa of the day before the race, when the rider for Poseidon, god of the seas, had been disqualified by Zeus, his brother, for cheating. Outraged, Poseidon had caused sea water to pour from the winged horse stables, washing away hay and saddlecloths alike. Bellerophon, the groom, insisted that Poseidon stop. But to no avail. At least the horses had been out grazing at the time.

Poseidon was surely behind the storm too, thought Pippa. Maybe he was mad at the mortals, or maybe it was a grudge with a god. She didn't know, but in either case, it couldn't be good. She glanced up at the sky, shielding her eyes from the rain with her hand, wondering if she could spy him—or Zeus. All she could see were the clouds, but . . . were those stars peeking through the clouds, against a dark sky? That didn't make sense. It was late but not yet nighttime.

The sight made her shiver.

That, and the fact that her hair was drenched, and her tunic too. Zeph kept stumbling on the slick ground, making it hard for her to keep her balance, especially when she turned backward to check on Tazo.

He was soaking as well, water dripping from his feathers, mane, and tail. He wasn't shivering . . . yet. But they had to hurry. He was hurt, and a hurt horse was more likely to become ill.

That worry was soon replaced by another. They were nearing the agora, and Pippa wasn't sure what to do. There was only one road through the town, and, although the market stalls would be closed up because of the storm, she still might meet someone—a lingering merchant, a homeless beggar. She didn't want anyone seeing the colt. Who knew how they would react? She wished she had a cloak or blanket to cover Tazo's wings.

First, though, they had to pass Leda's hut. And if *Leda* saw the colt, she would tell everyone. Perhaps if they cantered—galloped even—the old woman wouldn't recognize her or see Tazo's wings. But the colt was injured, and Pippa didn't want to strain him.

Just then, Pippa spotted something through the rain: an empty sack, hanging from an olive branch in Leda's garden, likely for carrying her vegetables to the market. Pippa glanced at the old woman's hut. The shutters were closed. This was her chance.

Quickly, she slipped off Zeph and tied Tazo's make-shift rope to the branch of a tree along the road. Then she hurried into the garden.

It was filled with flowering shrubs and trees heavy with almonds, apples, and figs. Herbs and vegetables—radishes and leeks, beans and cabbages—were bowed and beaten down from the storm. Pippa darted through the vegetables, grabbing the sack from the branch. She heard a noise—a creak like a door opening—and spun around, but the door and the shutters were closed. It must have been the storm. Still, she chastised herself.

How foolish, stopping and going right into the very spot she should have passed the quickest!

But now it was done. Hurrying back to the horses, she wrung out the sackcloth, even though she knew it would soon be soaked again, then draped it gently over Tazo's back, hiding his wings as best she could. He snorted and flinched, as though it was bothering his wing.

"Please, Tazo," she whispered. "It's the only way."

Tazo didn't seem to agree. His ears were back and he looked ready to bolt. But Zeph whinnied softly and nosed him. Tazo settled, though he still gave a shudder, and Pippa prayed to Aphrodite and Zeus again, this time that the cloth would stay on and that they'd make it through the town unnoticed.

Pippa untied Tazo and they kept going. This time she walked, leading the colt, Zeph following beside him. Her sandals slapped against her feet, water squishing between her toes.

The agora was quiet. No delicious smells or lyre music filled the air. No chatter or haggling. Everyone had covered their wares and hidden away. At least, almost everyone. One woman, wrapped in a cloak that hid most of her face, hurried down the street. Pippa held her breath, but the woman merely gave Pippa a nod and didn't stop. The sackcloth had worked.

At last, they reached the farm, its sign creaking in the wind: "Stables of the Seven Sisters." The name came from both the constellation and the seven daughters of Nikon and Helena. Pippa made it eight.

As Pippa passed through the open gates, the rope jerked. She glanced back. Tazo had frozen in place, except for his tail, which flicked back and forth.

"It's okay," she said. "Just a little farther and there'll be figs for you."

But Tazo refused to budge.

A moment later she knew why.

"There you are!" came Bas's voice. Pippa turned to see him, dressed in a cloak, striding along the path toward them. "You said you weren't going riding. Astrea said I shouldn't have believed you, that she'd be riding, if she could—"

He stopped. His eyes went wide as he took in the colt.

"I found him in the forest," explained Pippa.

"And you brought him here?"

"I didn't know what else to do."

"A wild colt followed *you*?!" Bas was incredulous.

He stood, mouth wide open.

"I can't just abandon him now. He's hurt, Bas. And—"

She was about to tell him about Tazo's wings, but Bas interrupted. "We have to get out of the rain. Come on."

"To your parents?" said Pippa. "I don't think we should. Bas, I've been trying to tell you something. He has—"

"No, we shouldn't tell my parents," continued Bas. "The rain, Pippa, it's cursed! It's destroying all the crops. Everyone's frantic."

"But where can we keep him while he heals?"

Pippa thought of the solution at the same time as Bas.

"The old stables!" they both exclaimed.

Bas led the way through the pasture. Tazo was reluctant to follow at first but soon became curious, sniffing and looking at everything.

Inside the old stables it was musty but dry and quiet, except for the soft *drip-drip-drip* of a leak in one corner and the whistle of wind through the window. The sweet smell of hay filled the air, although there wasn't much hay stored there now, only a few sheaves stacked on one side, hard to see in the dim light. An old wooden cistern lay upside down, and two small stalls took up the back. A long time ago, this had been Nikon's only stable, but Pippa found that hard to imagine, with the dozen horses he cared for now.

Once he was inside, Tazo seemed to like it. He shook his head, his mane showering Pippa with water droplets.

"Tazo!" she scolded, laughing.

But Bas wasn't laughing.

His mouth hung open.

"That's his name," Pippa explained.

Still Bas didn't respond. Instead, he pointed. A single silvery-gold feather had escaped from under the sackcloth and was drifting to the ground, glinting like a star in the darkness.

"Is that . . . Is he . . . ?" Bas stammered.

Pippa nodded. "That's what I was trying to tell you."

Slowly, she removed the sackcloth from Tazo's back. He liked that and shook again, his wings shimmering and rising up slightly like two slivers of moon. He gave a short, pleased snort.

"*A winged horse,*" breathed Bas. "Here. But how . . . ?"

"I don't know exactly," Pippa said. "I think his mother must be one of the wild mares. Maybe something happened to her during the storm. But Tazo *is*

Zeph's son. I'm certain. I can just tell. His coloring's the same, except the gold. I didn't know what to do, other than bring him here."

"A winged horse," Bas repeated incredulously.

"Yes," said Pippa, feeling like they'd wasted enough time, with two wet and cold horses to tend to. (Although Zeph seemed to have taken care of himself by finding the sheaves of hay.) "I think one of his wings is injured. He needs to be looked after."

"Yes, yes, of course."

Pippa draped Tazo's cloth over a beam, then wrung out her hair. While Bas fetched supplies, she settled the colt into a stall.

"I told Father I found you," Bas said when he returned. "He was happy to hear it."

"You didn't say . . . ," started Pippa.

"No, of course not," replied Bas. "Just that we were taking care of Zeph."

"Good," she replied. "You can't say *anything* to them, Bas, not until we figure out what to do."

Bas nodded solemnly.

Carefully, she rubbed Tazo down—his legs, his neck, and, as gently as she could, his wings too. Bas tried to keep him still while Pippa examined Tazo's wing.

The colt's wings were even more magical in the soft light from the oil lamp than they had been in the daylight. The feathers shimmered like real gold and were soft like rose petals, despite still being a bit damp.

Pippa touched the feathers as gently as she could. "Like your father's." She glanced over at Zeph. "Except his were bigger."

Tazo's ears flicked back, as though he didn't appreciate the comparison.

There was a deep cut, but the wing itself didn't seem broken. With fingers that could never master the loom but seemed built for this, Pippa cleaned the cut and tied a band of soft cloth around it, to keep it still and clear of infection. She didn't have any salt and vinegar to clean it, or alum, ivy root, and pitch to treat it, but she would find some tomorrow. All the while, as the rain thrummed against the roof, Bas kept Tazo distracted by feeding him figs. He liked them and would've eaten them until he was sick, as Astrea did with honey cakes.

"No more," said Pippa eventually. "He needs to eat properly."

So they fixed him a supper of barley and beans and

gave him some water, but not so much it would chill him. Then Pippa turned her attention to Zeph, who was waiting patiently in the other stall eating hay. He didn't want to leave. And neither did she.

"I can sleep here tonight," she said. "I can bring Zeph to the stables in the morning, so no one is suspicious."

"But what about you?" said Bas.

"Tell them I'm sleeping in the stables, that Zeph doesn't like the storm." It wasn't the first time Pippa had slept with the horses, but it was something Helena did not approve of, something a proper young woman would never do.

"But you're wet, and you must be hungry."

"I'll be fine," replied Pippa.

Bas shook his head but knew that it was impossible to argue.

"My parents *are* distracted by the storm," Bas said slowly. "I'll bring you supper."

"Thank you," she said.

Bas shook his head again, then gazed at Tazo, who was now suddenly asleep, his energy gone as quickly as it had come, his wings moving up and down in a steady, wavelike rhythm.

"What will we do with him?" added Bas.

"I don't know," Pippa replied. And that was the truth.

Winged horses weren't supposed to be in the mortal realm. Tazo had survived this long, but if anyone else saw him, what would happen? Who knew what others would do, if they knew a real winged horse lived below the mountain? And the gods, what would *they* do? She couldn't keep him, could she? She wanted nothing more.

"I can't believe it. I really can't believe it," murmured Bas.

Neither could Pippa. She didn't feel cold or hungry or tired. Only excited and—despite the strange and frightening storm—thankful.

Even more so when Bas returned with a plate of food. Her appetite returned at the sight and smell of the grilled fish, bread and cheese, and cup of watereddown wine.

"Helena wanted you to have this too," he said, passing her a clean peplos.

Just like Helena to think about her appearance.

Still, once Bas was gone, it felt nice to change into the clean, dry clothing. And, as she ate, guilt rose in Pippa. Helena and Nikon had given her so much—a home, food, and care. She *could* try harder.

Yet, when she finally fell asleep to the lullaby of the swishing tails and the rumble of rain, like a thousand hoofbeats, her dreams weren't filled with nightmares of being tangled in yarn. They were filled with flying, on a horse with wings that lit the sky, bright as the moon.

Five

Pippa was woken, not by the storm—but by voices. Loud ones, drifting in from outside.

She jolted up from her spot on the floor beside Zeph. Zeph was already awake, his ears pricked.

Was it day or night? Light streamed in through the window, but when Pippa looked up through it, she saw that the clouds had disappeared and the sky was filled with stars, so many, so bright it seemed like they were woven together. Nyx, goddess of night, was certainly not tangled up in the storm now, and was putting on her best display.

If it was still night—or even early morning—why the voices? It sounded like half the village was gathered outside.

"My crops will be ruined!" came one.

"It's the gods. They must be mad at us," said another.

"But why?!" burst another voice, even louder. "Why are the gods so angry?"

"I told you, because of what is here. In these old stables. Show us, boy!"

This voice belonged to a woman. It seemed familiar, but Pippa couldn't identify the speaker. She didn't need to though, to feel the jolt of fear. The woman was talking about Tazo.

Tazo was awake now too, his wings slightly raised, glimmering in the dim light in the stables. His eyes shone, and his nostrils were flared wide with fright.

Pippa's hands shook as she frantically looked for something to hide him with.

But she didn't have time.

The doors flung open, letting in more starry light and the heavy smell of salt. Although Pippa had never been to the sea, she imagined this is what it smelled like.

Tazo gave a frightened snort, shying back, as the

crowd surged into the stables. Gasps and cries of surprise and shock filled the air.

Nikon stood up front, with a lantern, shaking his head in disbelief. Bas stood beside him, his face twisted in dismay.

How could he? Pippa's heart thumped with anger, but then his eyes met hers.

"I'm sorry," Bas mouthed, and he gave her such an apologetic look she knew this wasn't his doing.

It was Leda's. The crone hobbled forward, wheezing as she spoke. "A winged horse." She pointed at Tazo.

"Oh, Pippa, what have you done?" murmured Helena. Beside her, Astrea gasped.

The colt snorted and showed the whites of his eyes. His ears were flattened on his head, and his tail clamped down.

"*Shh.* It's okay. It's okay," Pippa soothed.

Pippa kept stroking and talking to him until, at last, Tazo's trembling stopped and he was quiet.

"Where did he come from? How did he get here?" came a villager's voice.

"The gods must have sent him," said another.

41

"No, can't you see? He's Zeph's," piped Astrea.

There was a collective murmuring. "The winged horse's colt . . . Can it be?"

"Zephyr's colt or not, it shouldn't be here." Leda's crackly voice silenced them. "Poseidon is in charge of the seas and all horses too. No wonder the salt water poured from the sky. Poseidon does not want *his* steed on mortal soil. He is punishing us for keeping it here." Leda glared at Nikon.

"I haven't seen the creature before now," Nikon cried, raising his hands in the air.

"No, perhaps not," replied Leda. Once again, she pointed accusingly at Pippa. "I saw *her* bring it back yesterday from the hills, during the storm."

Everyone stared at Pippa, and she felt her skin prickle under their gaze.

"I found him in the woods. He was hurt," Pippa explained, trying to keep her voice calm.

"And so you brought him here? And you didn't tell me?" said Nikon. He didn't seem angry, only full of astonishment. He turned to his son. "Basileus! You should have—"

"It's not Bas's fault. And the colt isn't doing any

harm . . . ," stammered Pippa.

"Harm?! He's a curse," spat Leda.

"A curse?" Pippa shook her head. "But he's just a colt. With wings. He's a gift."

"*Ha!*" Leda spat again. "Zephyr's son has the wings that he himself lost. You might see this as a gift. But I know the truth. I know a thing or two about curses."

Her fingers curled around the cloak covering her head, and she threw it back . . . to reveal gold!

Instead of the white locks of an old woman, her hair glistened in the lantern light, like Helena's finest brooch. Leda rapped it with her knuckles.

"Yes, it really is gold," she said. "Now you all know my secret. I am a descendant of the great King Midas."

Gasps and exclamations filled the old stable, as Leda went on.

"King Midas, as many of you know, had a lust for gold, so he asked the gods to grant him a golden touch. You don't ask things of the gods. You only give. But King Midas asked, and the gods granted his wish. At first, he saw it as a gift. Until he realized that *everything* he touched became gold: the food he wanted to eat, the water he wanted to drink, even his own daughter.

He begged to have the curse reversed. Luckily, the gods took pity on him and took it away." Leda paused. "Most of you know this story. But you don't know the rest. When his daughter was brought back to life, her hair was never the same. It remained gold. And her daughter's hair was gold, and her daughter's daughter. And now, mine."

"But golden hair, that's not a curse . . . ," said Helena.

"Not a curse!" Leda laughed. "You think it's a blessing to be weighed down day and night by this golden monstrosity? It has given me this hunch. This is what comes of meddling with the gods. This is why we must destroy the colt."

"*Destroy?!*" Pippa burst out.

Zeph pawed the earth, and Tazo snorted.

"Destroy?" Nikon also looked upset.

Leda softened her tone. "I meant, of course, take it to the temple. Poseidon's temple in Iolkos. The priest there will know what to do with it."

Leda didn't have to say what she was thinking. There was only one thing priests did in their temples: make sacrifices to the gods and goddesses.

"You can't!" cried Pippa.

"Hush," said Nikon. "Leda is right. The priest will

know what to do. It's a winged horse. It belongs with the gods."

"But . . . ," stammered Pippa.

"If we don't do something," said Leda, "there is no doubt more ill fortune will rage across our lands. Poseidon's anger knows no bounds. We have to take the colt to the temple—immediately!"

Right now? Pippa's stomach tightened.

Nikon nodded. "It is the gods' horse, not a mortal one, and Leda is right. If we don't take it to the temple, who knows what further disasters might befall us."

The villagers and farmers nodded and murmured their assent.

"Bas, make sure the colt is fed," ordered Nikon. "Hippolyta, prepare Zephyr. You will be coming with us."

"Can I . . . ," started Astrea.

Helena tugged her hand. "No, *we* are going back to the oikos."

"Yes," said Nikon. "Back to my courtyard. There is much to arrange."

"And breakfast to be eaten," added Helena. "No point leaving with empty stomachs."

* * *

"I'm so sorry, Pippa," Bas babbled, as he and Pippa led the horses toward the main stables. "It's not my fault. Leda woke us up. She forced me to tell."

"It's okay," said Pippa. Though of course, it wasn't. Not at all.

The crowd had already made its way across the field to the house, disappearing from sight into the courtyard. Only Astrea lingered, watching them from afar.

"You never know what the priestess might say," Bas went on. "Perhaps we *will* be able to keep him."

Pippa shook her head. "No, Bas. You know what will happen to him. I can't do it. Zeph would never forgive me. I could never forgive myself. I have to . . ."

The plan formed as she whispered it, as they stepped inside the cool, dry stables. Her voice echoed. "I have to take Tazo to the gods myself. To the winged horse stables on Mount Olympus."

Bas shuddered. Pippa knew that, unlike her, he had no good memories of the mountain. "But we were banished. You can't go back. Who knows what Zeus will do to you! Or to Zeph!"

"I won't take Zeph, I'll go on foot." Pippa took a deep breath. "I'll explain to Zeus and Poseidon why

Tazo was here. Then I'll come home."

"You're going to talk to Zeus?" Bas shook his head in disbelief. "Pippa, you're crazy!"

"I'm going to fix things, Bas. And I'm going to save Tazo too."

The colt, as if he understood, nickered beside her.

Bas shook his head again. "You can't do this, Pippa—"

"I have to!"

"—alone," finished Bas.

Pippa's eyes widened.

"I'll come with you. We can take one of my father's horses. It will be quicker."

Pippa knew how hard it was for him to suggest this, and her heart warmed.

"It's my fault everyone saw Tazo," he continued. "I should have said no to Leda. I don't know how, but I should have."

"Oh, Bas." Pippa took a deep breath. "You can't come with me. Tazo is my responsibility. I promise, I won't be gone long. Just . . . just delay your father from coming after me. And take care of Zeph. Please."

"But . . ."

"*Please.*"

Slowly, Bas nodded. "For you, Pippa."

While Bas found a sheepskin to hide Tazo's wings, Pippa held Zeph's nose in her hands and gave him a kiss. "I won't be gone long. I promise. I'll keep your feather close."

Zeph flicked his ears, his dark eyes gazing deep into hers, full of understanding. Tazo gave a little snort.

She didn't have time to collect more than a pocketful of figs and one other thing.

Her map. The map of Mount Olympus had been a gift from the Fates, woven of their magic threads. After the race, Pippa had tried to give it to Aphrodite to return for her, but the goddess insisted that Pippa might need it one day. Had Aphrodite known about *this* day?

Pippa took the map from its hiding space in Zeph's stall and tucked it into her peplos.

There was no time to change into more suitable clothes. Besides, she couldn't go into the house to get her chiton anyway, not without raising suspicion. So she ripped her peplos along the side. At least she could run now.

When she returned, she'd never rip her dresses. She'd do everything to become a proper young woman, just as she'd promised Helena.

That was another reason she wanted to go, a reason she hadn't shared with Bas. This time on the mountain, she'd find out the facts about her parents. She'd learn exactly what happened. Then, maybe she'd finally be able to put her past to rest and focus on what she needed to learn to be a proper young woman.

"If, for some reason, the map doesn't work and you get lost, remember, just look for the stars," Bas said. "The Pleiades."

"The Seven Sisters," said Pippa; that was the constellation's other name.

"Yes. The stars shine right above here, the Stables of the Seven Sisters, so you will always know how to find your way home." Then Bas gave her his cloak, along with a hug. "You'd *better* come back," he added. "My other sisters are great and all, but you're my very favorite."

Six

The stars still filled the sky from edge to edge, but Pippa did not pause to admire them. The grass along the road, soaked and salty, licked at her legs.

She wished she could ride Tazo, but he was still young, and she doubted he would let her. He was wild and untrained. So she ran, Tazo trotting beside her, the two of them connected only by the rope. Her heart pounded with fear.

Bas would find a way to delay his father and Leda and the rest of the villagers, but not for long. And she was certain they'd be riding when they set off after her.

"Zeus, protect us," she whispered. "Keep us safe."

She thought again of Leda's story. It was true. Meddling with the gods and goddesses rarely did anyone any good. Instead, a mortal could end up turned into an echo, or a laurel tree, or perhaps a bear. She'd heard the stories. She'd lived them. She remembered the rider Theodoros, whom, it was rumored, Zeus had turned into a fish because he and his patron god, Poseidon, had cheated during training for the race.

But she also remembered how Zeus had winked at her. How they shared a deep love of winged horses. Even if Poseidon had caused the storm, it was Zeus she needed to talk to. Zeus was ruler of the gods, including his brother the god of the sea, *and* he loved horses. She was sure once she spoke with Zeus and explained everything, he would make things right.

As long as she made it to him.

As the sun slowly rose, hardly clearing the horizon, the full extent of the damage was laid bare. The storm had pounded the gardens and fields flat. Water had even flooded the houses' open courtyards and crept into some of the low-lying outbuildings. But she didn't stop to stare.

Good thing too. They had just passed the empty

town when she heard the sound of distant hooves and shouting voices.

A search party was coming after her. She and Tazo would never escape now, not on foot!

Unless . . .

She gently tugged the sheepskin off Tazo's back. If she rode him, maybe there was a chance. She was about to mount, but the bandage on his wing made her hesitate. No, she couldn't do it. Not only had he never been ridden before, but he was still injured. What if she hurt him more?

She threw the sheepskin on the ground. There was no use for it now.

"Hurry!" Pippa urged, more to herself than the colt. She ran as fast as she could into the woods, Tazo beside her.

She led Tazo through the bushes, along an old windy path that no one followed anymore. It zigzagged this way and that, but Tazo didn't seem to mind. It was a shortcut to the next town and to the mountain beyond.

The shouts grew louder. "That way! Through the bush!"

She glanced back and thought she saw Nikon

through the green and brown branches.

The undergrowth ripped Pippa's peplos and scratched at her legs. She hardly noticed.

They were going to be caught before they even had started out.

She looked for anything—a place to hide, a cave or bushes. But there was nothing. Her panic grew. Desperately she searched in her pocket for the map, not that it would be any help. It didn't detail trails so low or far from the mountain. At least, it hadn't. . . .

Her eyes went wide. There was a symbol of roses on the map that hadn't been there before!

The map had expanded to include villages and forests far beyond the great mountain, including Thessaly! And *now*, near the very spot she was standing, was a symbol of roses! Yet there were no roses on the windy trails in these woods. At least, there *hadn't* been.

But that, like the map, had changed. When she looked up, between two trees, she saw a gateway made of twisted roses.

Roses! They had marked a special trail that Aphrodite had made just for her and Bas, to lead them home from the mountain.

Was Aphrodite helping her? Or maybe the Fates?

They had given her the map, after all. And it was made from their magic threads.

She didn't really care, couldn't really think, as she ducked through the roses, pulling Tazo after her . . . and emerged at the base of Mount Olympus—grand, glorious, and capped with clouds.

She turned around, fearing Nikon and the others would follow through, but the gateway . . . was gone. The shouts and sound of hooves were gone too.

There was only the sound of birds and wind, and . . . crying?

She froze and tried to keep Tazo still. But before she had a chance to hide, a face peered around the trunk of a tree at her. A boy!

He looked puffy and pale, and his eyes were red. His dark brown hair fell like a tangled mane. He didn't look much older than her, but it was hard to tell, even when he came to stand in front of her, because he was wearing a huge cloak. It was a lion's pelt, with the head still attached. But despite its size, it looked ragged, as though it was very, very old.

"Are you okay?" Pippa asked, standing up, forgetting for a moment that Tazo was uncovered.

But the boy didn't seem to notice.

"*Okay?*" he said, rubbing his eyes. "Of course I'm okay. It's you I was worried about. You must be lost. This is the way up the mountain. It's only for us heroes to attempt."

"Heroes?" Pippa raised her eyebrows.

"Yes, heroes," said the boy. "Don't you know who I am?" He pulled himself up to his full height—which was not any taller than Pippa.

"No," replied Pippa.

The boy huffed scornfully. "Typical. I shouldn't be surprised. You *are* just a girl."

"Just a girl? Don't you know—" started Pippa, about to tell him who *she* was, that she had been one of the riders in the great Winged Horse Race. But then she remembered that proper girls weren't supposed to climb mountains, especially not on their own, when the boy interrupted.

"For your information, my name is Hero."

"Hero?"

Tazo snorted. Pippa glanced at the boy, thinking he would look at the horse and notice his wings, but he didn't.

Even though Tazo was standing right next to him and, much to Pippa's surprise, nosing his cloak. Tazo wasn't even that friendly with Bas.

Still, Hero didn't pay the horse any attention. "My name is Hero because that is exactly what I am: a hero. The great Oracle herself said so and for good reason. My ancestor was the legendary Hercules."

Hercules! Pippa had heard of him, of course. Everyone had. Hercules was a great hero who had killed the dreaded nine-headed serpent, the Hydra. He had wrestled the fearsome Cretan bull and captured the golden-horned deer of Ceryneia. And, in what was once her favorite of his deeds, he had cleaned King Augeas's stables—the largest, dirtiest stables in Greece—in a single day by redirecting a river through them. Mind you, now that Pippa had actually seen what such a flood could do, she wasn't so sure this was the best method. It just meant more cleaning.

She must have been frowning at this thought, for Hero burst out, "Oh, so you don't believe me?"

"No. I didn't say that," said Pippa taken aback.

"This proves that I am!" Hero tugged at his cloak. "This is the fur of the Nemean lion, the most fearsome lion ever known, slain by Hercules himself!" He slung the cloak back with a flourish, and it hit Tazo in the nose.

Tazo snorted again, and at last Hero noticed him. "Watch out, hors . . . ," Hero began. Then he caught sight of Tazo's wings and gulped. "A *winged* horse."

"You must be used to seeing magical animals, being a hero. Right?" Pippa prodded.

"Of . . . of course," replied Hero, though his eyes never left Tazo's wings.

"Well, my winged horse and I had better get going," said Pippa. "Good luck."

She tugged Tazo away, though Tazo seemed reluctant to come, still too interested in Hero.

"Wait!" said Hero. "Where are you going?"

"Up the mountain of course."

"Well, so am I. *I* can take you," declared Hero.

"Thank you, but I don't need your help."

Hero shook his head. "You're wrong. The gods and goddesses are mad. Didn't you see the storm? That's why I'm heading up Mount Olympus. I want to find out what's happening and make sure there are no more storms. I'm going to save everyone. You'd better come with me. I can look out for you."

"I'm fine on my own," said Pippa stoutly.

But too late. Hero had already taken the lead, with Tazo trotting happily behind. The rope in Pippa's hand grew taut, and she had no choice but to follow.

Seven

Pippa had never been very talkative. She preferred the silence of horses and the shimmer of stars at night. In her lonely life as a foundling, the constellations had been her only constant companions.

Bas was also quiet, no doubt a result of living with seven sisters.

But not Hero.

"I have always had a good sense of direction," he babbled, walking in the completely *wrong* direction. "Why, when I was only three, I walked all the way from the market to our oikos by myself."

Pippa took a different route, and Hero added, "Ah, yes, that way. I knew it was that way. I was going to suggest we turn up ahead. But we can turn now, if you'd rather."

"I'd rather," said Pippa shortly.

"I'm an excellent hunter too," Hero went on. "I trained with Orion's sword. Orion, the great hunter—the one honored in the sky as a constellation. And my father said Artemis herself, goddess of the hunt, watched over me when I was still a baby. I suppose your father brags similarly of you. It's what parents do, right?" Hero said, almost questioningly.

Pippa felt a pang. Of course she didn't know. Before she could explain, Hero went on.

"I even fought off two snakes in my cradle, just like Hercules."

"Really?" said Pippa doubtfully. "So you'll be able to catch us some supper?"

Hero paused, then laughed. "On the mountain? You can't *hunt* on the mountain. I wouldn't want to make the gods angry. Not when they already are."

"Right," said Pippa, unconvinced.

She needed to get rid of him. But what if he really did have some connection with the gods? That might help her. He did seem to have a connection to Tazo, or at least, Tazo had connected to him. Tazo was trotting right beside him. It didn't make any sense to Pippa, but sometimes you just couldn't explain the actions of horses. Except Zeph. He and Pippa understood each other so well.

She missed Zeph and touched his feather. The feather *was* longer than Tazo's, but—glancing over at the colt—surprisingly not by much.

Tazo's wings and feathers were truly remarkable. Did it have something to do with his being born of a regular and a winged horse? She wasn't sure. Although it had only been a night and a day, his wing looked like it was already healing well. His bandage had fallen off during their escape and it looked like she didn't need to replace it. Yet he still didn't seem interested in flying. She hadn't even seen him fully stretch his wings. It was as if he wasn't certain that he was a winged horse at all. He was much more interested in exploring the world on the ground.

Maybe the winged horse stables *was* the right place for him. The grooms could help him learn to use his wings. But Pippa already dreaded the day she'd have to say goodbye.

By the time night fell, after hours of Hero's jabbering, Pippa was renewed in her determination to leave him. She planned to wait until he fell asleep and then sneak off with Tazo. Unfortunately, Hero talked and talked until she fell asleep instead!

Luckily, she woke up before he did. It was early morning, and the stars once again filled the sky brighter and fuller than ever, casting a blueish light over the mountainside. Without Hero's chatter, it was silent, almost ominously so.

Tazo was sleeping and swaying unsteadily. She gave him a gentle rub on his nose, and his eyes flicked open, displeased. It took a piece of honey cake that she'd pocketed from the night before to convince him to follow her.

At last, they started out.

But they didn't get far.

They were emerging from the tree line and entering rocky meadows, when Pippa heard Hero's unmistakable voice: "Pippa! Where are you?"

Pippa scoured the area for a place to hide, and, to her luck, spotted just the thing. A humongous statue, so big it was like a mini mountain itself. It was hard to make out at first because it was so large and it had been tipped over onto its side. When Pippa tilted her head, she could see it was Poseidon, carved in marble, a giant trident in one hand and a lightning bolt in the other. There was nothing particularly strange about a giant statue of a god. Gods loved their statues! But . . . *Lightning bolts are Zeus's weapons.*

Pippa couldn't think on it for long though. The space between the bolt and his arm made a perfect hollow to hide, and she pulled Tazo in at once.

"Shhh," she hushed.

"Pippa?!" Hero's voice came once again, this time sounding strained. "If you're looking for breakfast, you don't need to. I brought plenty of honey cakes."

She felt bad—but only a little. This was *her* adventure. She had met this boy only yesterday.

She peeked through a crack in the marble, watching him emerge from the trees, when she noticed something that made her heart jump.

Hero wasn't the only one at the forest's edge!

There, perched in a twisted tree, was a creature she'd heard of but never seen. A creature she and Tazo must have passed under only moments before. A siren!

Half woman, half bird, sirens used their magical voices to lure humans, usually sailors, to their deaths.

But this siren was nowhere near the sea.

She sat on a bent branch, her claws curled around it tightly. Her crooked wings were the color of stormy gray waves and covered in white speckles. Her human face was partially hidden in shadows. Still, Pippa could make out enough to be terrified: a large nose, almost like a beak; a toothy mouth, open in a snore. *At least she's sleeping.*

But with the noise that Hero was making, she wouldn't be for long.

"Pippa?" he called again.

The boy looked surprisingly small, even wearing his lion's pelt.

Pippa couldn't help herself. She leaned out of the statue's hollow. "Hero! Shh!" She pointed up to the siren.

Hero didn't understand at all. Instead, he smiled, gave a big wave and shouted, *extra* loudly, "*There* you are!"

"*No . . . ,*" started Pippa.

Too late.

The siren's eyes snapped open. She opened her wings, making a whooshing sound like the crash of waves on the shore.

Hero turned.

Pippa couldn't see his reaction, but she could imagine it.

"Hero, here! Hide!" she cried.

Hero snapped his attention back to her. He didn't hesitate. He ran, tripping over his cloak, and dove into the statue's hollow, out of sight, just as the siren let out a note, the most compelling note Pippa had ever heard.

"Cover your ears!" cried Pippa.

Hero did. Tazo's ears flicked back and forth.

Pippa didn't know whether to cover her ears or the colt's. Sirens' voices didn't affect horses, did they? She didn't know. But she didn't need to decide. The siren's song was finished with just the single note. She wasn't interested in what she couldn't see. She circled in the air—once, twice—then took off, rising up into the sea of the sky.

When the siren was out of sight, Pippa breathed a sigh of relief. Hero snorted, along with Tazo, though the boy looked pale.

"What is a siren doing *here*?" Pippa murmured.

"It's because of Poseidon," said Hero in a know-it-all voice.

"But why?" said Pippa.

Hero didn't have an answer to that.